# THE
# ANIMAL
## Picture Word Book

**Claudia Zeff**

**Illustrated by Nick Price**

**Consultant: Betty Root**

# By the pond

water vole

snail

reeds

kingfisher

otter

frog

water lily

pond weed

4 newt

swan

maggots

minnows

swallow

frog's eggs

tadpole

net

harvest mouse

grebe

water shrew

heron

wren

pike

stickleback    grasshopper    dragonfly    ducklings    duck

5

# On the seashore

gull

tern

plover

oyster-catcher

seaweed

limpets

periwinkles

pebbles

blenny

sand eel

sea anemone

sea urchin

starfish

oyster

barnacles

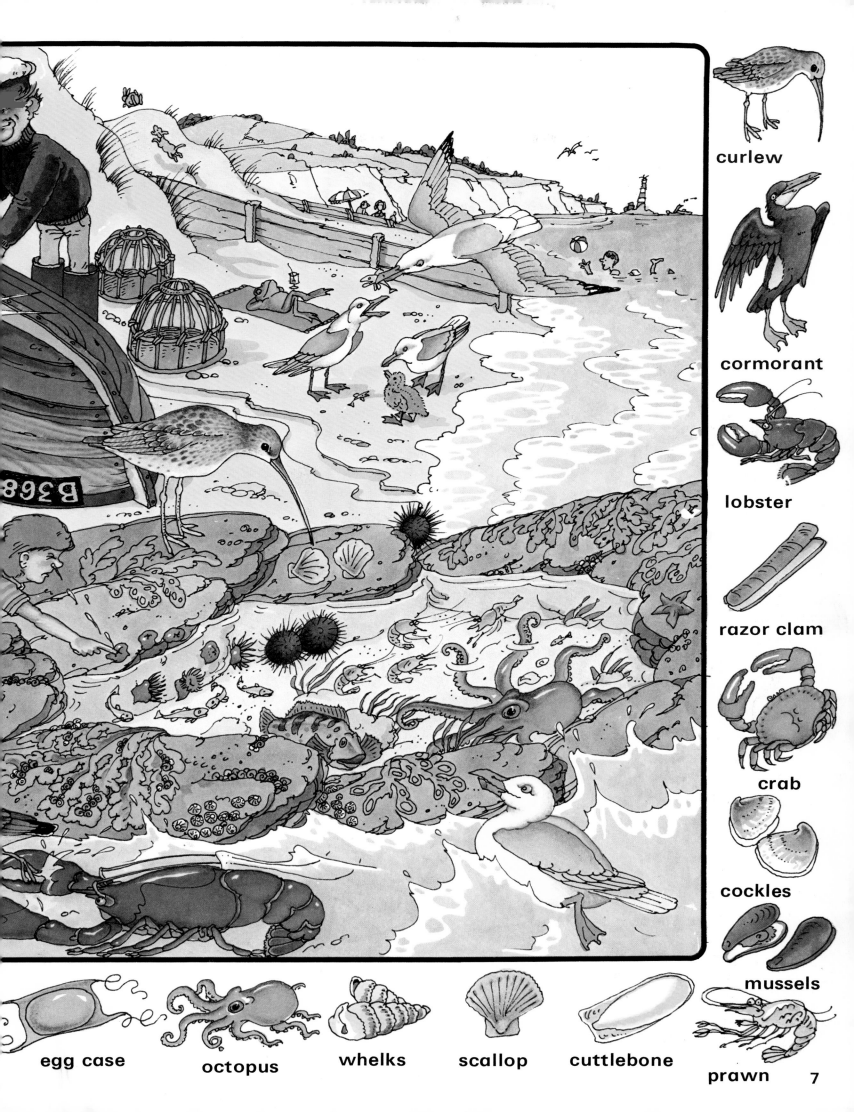

curlew

cormorant

lobster

razor clam

crab

cockles

mussels

egg case

octopus

whelks

scallop

cuttlebone

prawn

# In the mountains

chipmunk

moose

wolf

elk

raccoon

porcupine

black bear

8

beaver

mink

skunk

red fox

cave

mountain goat

grizzly bear

puma

salmon

quail

maple tree

berries

marmot

woodchuck

bighorn sheep

pine cones

eagle

wild turkey

9

# In the sea

coral

eel

parrot fish

sponge

puffer fish

sea squirt

scorpion fish

angler fish

angel fish

10    barracuda

giant clam

sun-fish

manta ray

stone fish

dolphin

shark

skate

swordfish

turtle

flying fish

jellyfish

sea horse

sawfish

cuttlefish

aqualung

diver

hippopotamus

python

elephant

zebra

bustard

termites' nest

water buffalo

lion cub

At the waterhole

12    lion

gnu

lioness

hyena

flamingo

gazelle

crane

giant anteater

nest

weaver bird

baobob tree

pelican

wart hog

giraffe

acacia tree

rhinoceros

jackal

baboon

cheetah

13

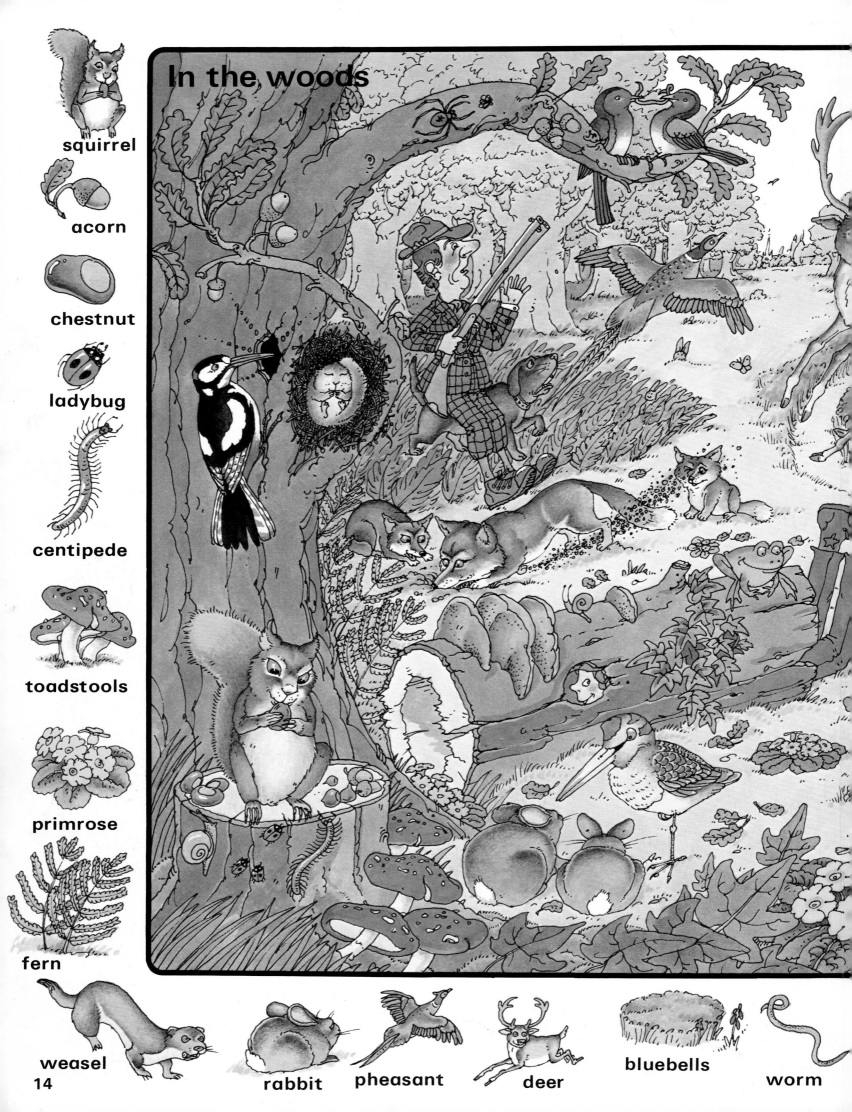

# In the woods

squirrel

acorn

chestnut

ladybug

centipede

toadstools

primrose

fern

weasel

14

rabbit

pheasant

deer

bluebells

worm

dormouse

woodpecker

butterfly

mistletoe

mole

molehill

woodcock

crow

robin

fox

badger

oak tree

15

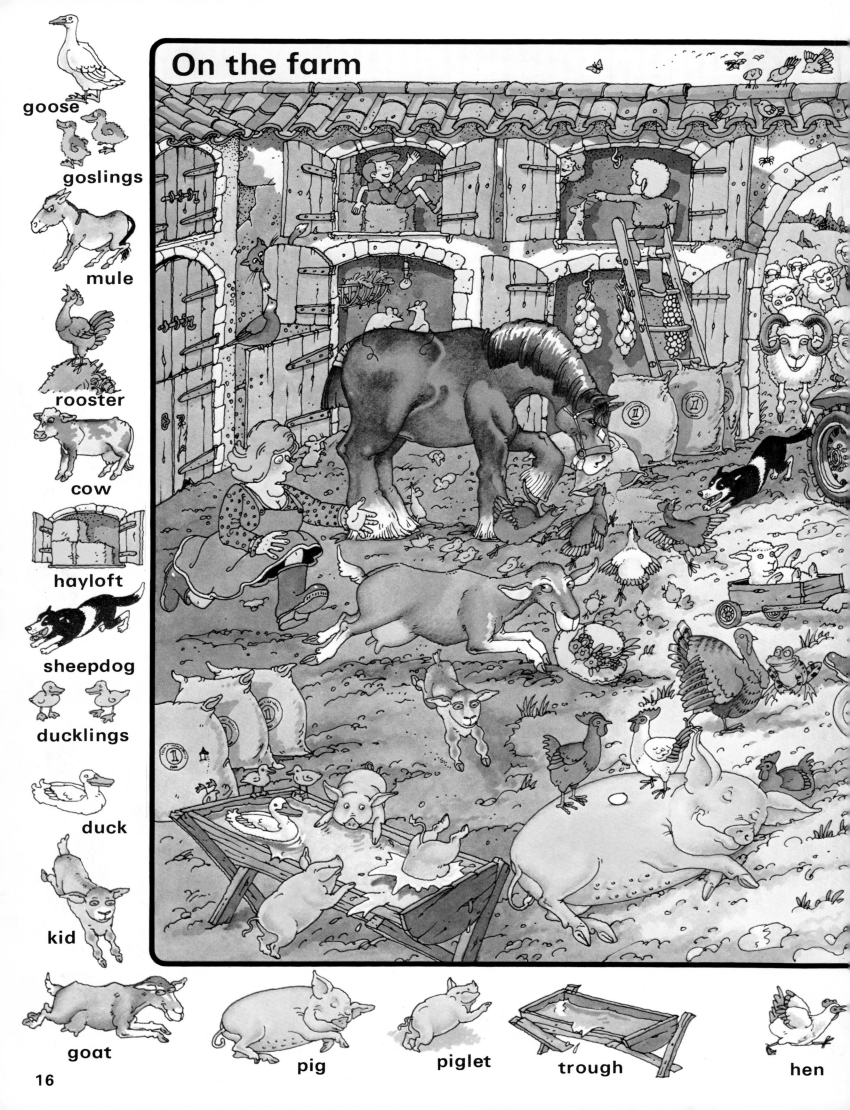

# On the farm

goose

goslings

mule

rooster

cow

hayloft

sheepdog

ducklings

duck

kid

goat

pig

piglet

trough

hen

16

bull

turkey

tractor

ram

lamb

sheep

bales of hay

chicks

cat

work horse

cowshed

sack of corn

stable

17

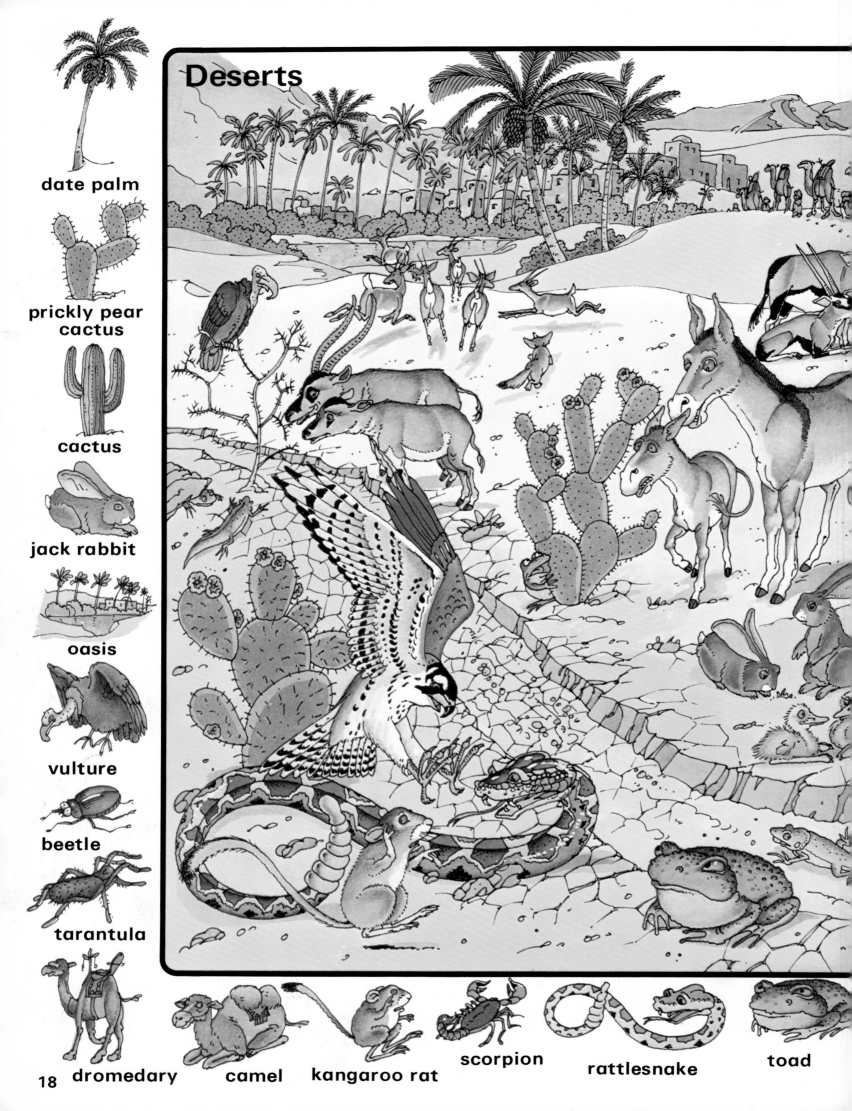

# Deserts

date palm

prickly pear cactus

cactus

jack rabbit

oasis

vulture

beetle

tarantula

dromedary

camel

kangaroo rat

scorpion

rattlesnake

toad

18

ostrich

ostrich egg

fennec fox

hawk

owl

nomad

bobcat

foal

donkey

addax

oryx

banana tree

cocoa tree

armadillo

spider monkey

boa constrictor

okapi

jaguar

gorilla

# In the jungle

opossum

lemur

chimpanzee

fruit bat

pineapple plant

egret

scarlet ibis

20

creeper

gibbon

orang utan

hummingbird

sloth

toucan

bird of paradise

parrot    crocodile    spoonbill    iguana    loris    bamboo

# In frozen lands

seal

seal pup

arctic fox

albatross

puffin

reindeer

musk ox

whale

walrus

ermine

ptarmigan

iceberg

22

snowy owl

polar bear

lemmings

tern

husky dog

penguin

penguin chick

igloo

kayak

sled

spear

Eskimo

23

# In Australia

tiger snake

frilled lizard

dingo

finch

joey

kangaroo

emu

emu eggs

24  wombat

emu chick

koala bear

cub

lyrebird

parakeet

wallaby

echidna

rabbit

gum tree

aborigine

eucalyptus
tree

boomerang

platypus

bandicoot

kookaburra

cockatoo

stick
insect

25

# At the dog show

greyhound

Pekingese

beagle

Irish setter

dachshund

Scottish terrier

St Bernard

Dobermann pinscher

26  bulldog

boxer

Labrador retriever

poodle

Dalmatian

hare

borzoi

cocker spaniel

Old English sheepdog

corgi

Afghan hound

Great Dane

pug

whippet     bloodhound     Pyrenean mountain dog     German shepherd     chow     basset hound

27

# At the pet store

puppy

kitten

hamster

gerbil

tortoise

guinea pig

rabbit

parrot

myna bird

canary

parakeet

goldfish

tropical fish

silk worms

kennel

28

aquarium

birdcage

perch

dog biscuits

leash

collar

straw

basket

Siamese cat

blue Persian cat

monkey

doves

fish bowl

29

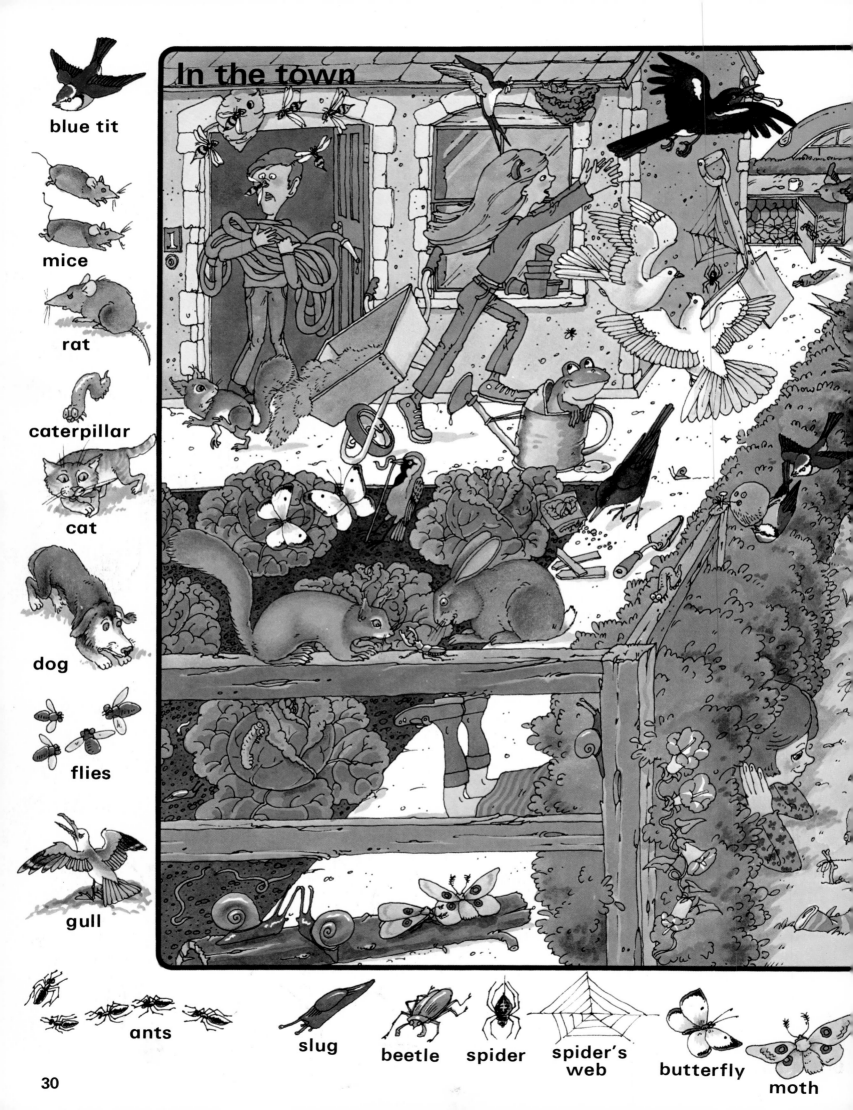

# In the town

blue tit

mice

rat

caterpillar

cat

dog

flies

gull

ants

slug

beetle

spider

spider's web

butterfly

moth

starling

house martin

hedgehog

rabbit

squirrel

sparrow

wasps

wasps' nest

blackbird        magpie        worms        pigeon        owl

31

# Animal families

stallion (father)

mare (mother)

foal

buck (father)

baby rabbit

doe (mother)

ram (father)

ewe (mother)

lamb

rooster (father)

hen (mother)

chick

drake (father)

duck (mother)

duckling

nanny (mother)

billy (father)

kid

sow (mother)

piglet

boar (father)

peacock (father)

buck (father)

doe (mother)

chick

peahen (mother)

fawn

fox (father)

bull (father)

cow (mother)

vixen (mother)

calf

fox cub

dog (father)

tom (father)

cat (mother)

bitch (mother)

puppy

kitten

cob (father)

goose (mother)

gosling

gander (father)

pen (mother)

cygnet

# Animal words

tail

hump

beak

tongue

antlers

trunk

claws

tusk

mane

webbed foot

horns

fleece

quills

hoof

34

whiskers

wing

teeth

talons

ear

neck

pouch

leg

snout

fin

shell

eye

paw

feathers

scales

fur

# Animal homes

rabbits' burrow

storks' nest

anthill

beehive

bears' den

flamingo's nest

squirrel's nest

eagles' eyrie

beavers' lodge

# Animal groups

skein of ducks

pride of lions

pack of hounds

school of whales

flight of birds

swarm of locusts

herd of cows

flock of sheep

gaggle of geese

shoal of mackerel

# Story book animals

phoenix

demon

winged horse

sea monster

roc

unicorn

mermaid

dragon

centaur

# Nighttime animals

bat

mongoose

fireflies

kiwi

hyena

moth

rat

bush baby

owl

badger

cricket

mouse

pangolin

loris

# Animals of long ago

dodo

woolly mammoth

cave bear

quagga

Tasmanian wolf

woolly rhinoceros

moa

sabre toothed cat

giant sloth

# Dinosaurs

kentrosaurus

spinosaurus

tyrannosaurus rex

anatosaurus

paleoscincus

pteranodon

stegosaurus

triceratops

plesiosaurus

diplodocus

iguanodon

# Words in order

This is a list of all the words in the pictures. They are in the same order as the alphabet. After each word is a number. On that page you will find the word and a picture.

## a

aborigine, 25
acacia tree, 13
acorn, 14
addax, 19
Afghan hound, 27
albatross, 22
Alsatian dog, 27
anatosaurus, 41
anemone, sea, 6
angel fish, 10
angler fish, 10
animal families, 32 and 33
animal groups, 37
animal homes, 36
animal words, 34 and 35
animals of long ago, 40
ant, 30
anteater, giant, 13
anthill, 36
antler, 34
aqualung, 11
aquarium, 29
arctic fox, 22
armadillo, 20
at the dogshow, 26 and 27
at the petshop, 28 and 29
at the pond, 4 and 5
at the waterhole, 12 and 13

## b

baboon, 13
baby rabbit, 32
badger, 15, 39
bale of hay, 17
bamboo, 21
banana tree, 20
bandicoot, 25
baobob tree, 13
barnacle, 6
barracuda, 10
basket, cat, 29
basset hound, 27
bat, 39
bat, fruit, 20
beagle, 26
beak, 34
bear, 8
bear, black, 8
bear, cave, 40
bear, grizzly, 9
bear, koala and cub, 24
bear, polar, 23
bears' den, 36
beaver, 8
beavers' lodge, 36
beehive, 36
beetle, 18, 30
berry, 9
bighorn sheep, 9
billy goat, 32
birds:
   albatross, 22
   bird of paradise, 21
   blackbird, 31
   blue tit, 30
   bustard, 12
   canary, 28
   cockatoo, 25
   cormorant, 7
   crane, 13
   curlew, 7
   dodo, 40
   dove, 29
   duck, 5, 32
   eagle, 9
   egret, 20
   emu, 24

   finch, 24
   flamingo, 12
   goose, 16, 33
   grebe, 5
   gull, 6
   hen, 16, 32
   heron, 5
   house martin, 31
   hummingbird, 21
   kingfisher, 4
   kiwi, 39
   kookaburra, 25
   lyrebird, 24
   magpie, 31
   moa, 40
   mynah bird, 28
   ostrich, 19
   owl, 19, 31, 39
   oystercatcher, 6
   parakeet, 24, 28
   parrot, 21
   peacock, 33
   pheasant, 14
   phoenix, 38
   pigeon, 31
   plover, 6
   ptarmigan, 22
   puffin, 22
   quail, 9
   robin, 15
   roc, 38
   scarlet ibis, 20
   snowy owl, 23
   sparrow, 31
   spoonbill, 21
   starling, 31
   stork, 36
   swallow, 4
   swan, 4
   tern, 6, 23
   toucan, 21
   turkey, 17
   vulture, 19
   weaver bird, 13
   wild turkey, 9
   woodcock, 15
   woodpecker, 15
   wren, 5
bird of paradise, 21
birdcage, 29
birds, flight of, 37
bitch (dog), 33
black bear, 8

blackbird, 31
blenny fish, 6
bloodhound, 27
blue Persian cat, 29
blue tit, 30
bluebell, 14
boa constrictor, 20
boar (pig), 32
bobcat, 19
boomerang, 25
borzoi, 27
boxer dog, 26
buck (deer), 33
buck (rabbit), 32
buffalo, water, 12
bull, 17, 33
bulldog, 26
burrow (rabbits'), 36
bush baby, 39
bustard, 12
butterfly, 15, 30

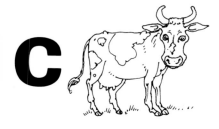

**c**

cactus, 18
cactus, prickly pear, 18
calf, 33
camel, 18
canary, 28
cat, 17, 30, 33
cat (kitten), 33
cat (tom), 33
cat basket, 29
cat, blue Persian, 29
cat, sabre-toothed, 40
cat, Siamese, 29
caterpillar, 30
cave, 8
cave bear, 40
centaur, 38
centipede, 14
cheetah, 13
chestnut, 14
chick, 17, 32
chick, emu, 24
chick, peacock, 33
chick, penguin, 23
chimpanzee, 20

chipmunk, 8
chow 27
clam, giant, 10
claw, 34
cob (swan), 33
cockatoo, 25
cocker spaniel, 27
cockle, 7
cocoa tree, 20
collar, 29
coral, 10
corgi, 27
cormorant, 7
corn, sack of, 17
cow, 16, 33
cows, herd of, 37
cowshed, 17
crab, 7
crane, 13
creeper, 21
cricket, 39
crocodile, 21
crow, 15
cub, fox, 33
cub, koala bear, 24
cub, lion, 12
curlew, 7
cuttlebone, 7
cuttlefish, 11
cygnet (swan), 33

**d**

dachshund, 26
Dalmatian dog, 26
date palm, 18
deer, 14
deer (buck), 33
deer (doe), 33
deer (fawn), 33
demon, 38
den, bears', 36
deserts, 18 and 19
dingo, 24
dinosaurs, 41

diplodocus, 41
diver, 11
Dobermann pinscher, 26
dodo, 40
doe (deer), 33
doe, (rabbit), 32
dog, 30, 33
dog (bitch), 33
dog (puppy), 33
dogs:
    Afghan hound, 27
    basset hound, 27
    beagle, 26
    bloodhound, 27
    borzoi, 27
    boxer, 26
    bulldog, 26
    chow 27
    cocker spaniel, 27
    corgi, 27
    dachshund, 26
    Dalmatian, 26
    Dobermann pinscher, 26
    German shepherd, 27
    Great Dane, 27
    greyhound, 26
    husky, 23
    Irish setter, 26
    Labrador retriever, 26
    Old English sheepdog, 27
    Pekingese, 26
    poodle, 26
    pug, 27
    Pyrenean mountain dog, 27
    St Bernard, 26
    Scottish terrier, 26
    sheepdog, 16
    whippet, 27
dog biscuit, 29
dogshow, 26 and 27
dolphin, 11
donkey, 19
dormouse, 15
dove, 29
dragon, 38
dragonfly, 5
drake (duck), 32
drey (squirrel's), 36
dromedary, 18
duck, 5, 32
duck (drake), 32
duckling, 5, 16, 32
ducks, skein of, 37

# e

eagle, 9
eagles' eyrie, 36
ear, 35
echidna, 25
eel, 10
eel, sand, 6
egg case, 7
egg, emu, 24
egg, ostrich, 19
egret, 20
elephant, 12
elk, 8
emu, 24
emu chick, 24
emu egg, 24
ermine, 22
Eskimo, 23
eucalyptus tree, 25
ewe (sheep), 32
eye, 35
eyrie (eagles'), 36

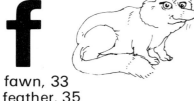

# f

fawn, 33
feather, 35
fennec fox, 19
fern, 14
fin, 35
finch, 24
firefly, 39
fish:
   angel fish, 10
   angler fish, 10
   barracuda, 10
   blenny, 6
   cuttlefish, 11
   dolphin, 11
   eel, 10
   flying fish, 11
   goldfish, 28
   jellyfish, 11

   mackerel, 37
   manta ray, 10
   minnow, 4
   parrot fish, 10
   pike, 5
   puffer fish, 10
   salmon, 9
   sand eel, 6
   sawfish, 11
   scorpion fish, 18
   shark, 11
   skate, 11
   starfish, 6
   stickleback, 5
   stonefish, 10
   sunfish, 10
   swordfish, 11
   tropical fish, 28
   whale, 22
fish bowl, 29
flamingo, 12
flamingos' nest, 36
fleece, 34
flies, 30
flight of birds, 37
flock of sheep, 37
fly, 30
flying fish, 11
foal (donkey), 19
foal (horse), 32
fox, 15, 33
fox (vixen), 33
fox cub, 33
fox, arctic, 22
fox, fennec, 19
fox, red, 15
frilled lizard, 24
frog, 4
frog's eggs, 4
fruit bat, 20
fur, 35

# g

gaggle of geese, 37
gazelle, 13
gerbil, 28
German shepherd, 27
giant anteater, 13
giant clam, 10

giant sloth, 40
gibbon, 21
giraffe, 13
gnu, 12
goat, 32
goat (kid), 16
goat, billy, 32
goat, mountain, 9
goat, nanny, 32
goldfish, 28
goose, 16, 33
goose (gander), 33
goose (gosling), 16, 33
gorilla, 20
grasshopper, 5
Great Dane, 27
grebe, 5
greyhound, 26
grizzly bear, 9
guinea pig, 28
gull, 6, 30
gum tree, 25

# h

hamster, 28
hare, 26
harvest mouse, 5
hawk, 19
hay loft, 16
hay, bales of, 17
hedgehog, 31
hen, 16, 32
herd of cows, 37
heron, 5
hippopotamus, 12
hoof, 34
horn, 34
horse (foal), 32
horse (mare), 32
horse (stallion), 32
**horse, winged** 38
horse, sea, 10
hounds, pack of, 37
house martin, 31
hummingbird, 21
hump, 34
husky dog, 23
hyena, 12, 39

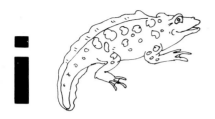

owl, snowy, 23
oyster, 6
oystercatcher, 6
ox, musk, 22

# p

pack of hounds, 37
paleoscincus, 41
palm, date, 18
pangolin, 39
parakeet, 24, 28
parrot, 21
parrot fish, 10
paw, 35
peacock, 33
peacock chick, 33
peahen, 33
pebble, 6
Pekingese, 26
pelican, 13
pen (swan), 33
penguin, 23
penguin chick, 23
perch (bird's), 29
periwinkle, 6
pheasant, 14
phoenix, 38
pig, 16
pig (boar), 32
pig (sow), 32
pig, guinea, 28
pigeon, 31
piglet, 16, 32
pike, 5
pine cone, 9
pineapple plant, 20
platypus, 25
plesiosaurus, 41
plover, 6
polar bear, 23
pond weed, 4
porcupine, 8
pouch (kangaroo), 35
prawn, 7

prickly pear cactus, 18
pride of lions, 37
primrose, 14
ptarmigan, 22
pteranodon, 41
puffer fish, 10
puffin, 22
pug dog, 27
puma, 9
pup, seal, 22
puppy, 33
Pyrenean mountain dog, 27
python, 12

# q

quagga, 40
quail, 9
quills, 34

# r

rabbit, 14, 25, 32
rabbit, (baby), 32
rabbit (buck), 32
rabbit (doe), 32
rabbits' burrow, 36
raccoon, 8
ram (sheep), 17, 32
rat, 30
rat, kangaroo, 18
rattlesnake, 18
razor clam, 7
red fox, 8
red squirrel, 14, 31
reeds, 4
reindeer, 22
rhinoceros, 13
rhinoceros, woolly, 40
robin, 15
roc, 38
rooster, 16, 32

# s

sabre toothed cat, 40
sack of corn, 17
St Bernard dog, 26
salmon, 9
sand eel, 6
sawfish, 11
scales (fish), 35
scallop, 7
scarlet ibis, 20
school of whales, 37
scorpion, 18
scorpion fish, 10
Scottish terrier, 26
sea anemone, 6
sea horse, 10
sea monster, 38
sea squirt, 10
sea urchin, 6
seal, 22
seal pup, 22
seaweed, 6
shark, 11
sheep, 17
sheep (ewe), 32
sheep (lamb), 17, 32
sheep (ram), 32
sheep, bighorn, 9
sheep, flock of, 37
sheepdog, 16
shell, razor, 7
shell (snail's), 35
shoal of mackerel, 37
Siamese cat, 29
silk worm, 28
skate, 11
skein of ducks, 37
skunk, 8
sled, 23
sloth, 21
sloth, giant, 40
slug, 30
snail, 4
snake (boa constrictor), 20
snake (python), 12
snake (rattlesnake), 18